THANK YOU FOR THE TADPOLE

by

Pat Thomson

Illustrated by

Mary Rayner

Delacorte Press/New York

Dad, I've got good news.
I'm going to Becky's
birthday party on Saturday.

Lucky you.
Are you going to bring a present?

Yes, but what can I bring her?
What can I bring for a present?
You tell me some things
and I'll make a list.

Well, now. Let me think.
Bring a tiny tadpole.

A tadpole?
Oh Dad, you are silly.
She wouldn't say thank you
for a tadpole,
and you can't put it in a box.
What else can I bring?

Let me think again.
Bring an enormous elephant.

An elephant?
Oh Dad, you are silly.
An elephant is too big.
It would get stuck in the door.
What else can I bring?

I must think even harder.
Bring an angry alligator.

An alligator?
Oh Dad, you are silly.
Alligators are dangerous.
It would eat the birthday cake,
and it might eat us.
What else can I bring?

I suppose I had better think
of something nice.
Bring a single swan.

A swan?
Oh Dad, you are silly.
Even one swan is too many,
and swans like to live on water.
What else can I bring?

This is getting difficult.
What can I think of next?
I know.
Bring an energetic eel.

An eel?
Oh Dad, you are silly.
They'd have to keep it in the bath
and that would frighten visitors.
What else can I bring?

I've got it.
This is really good.
Bring a terrible Tyrannosaurus Rex.

A Tyrannosaurus Rex?
That's a good idea.
But where do you get them from?
It's a difficult present to get.
Can you think of anything else?

Well I don't think I can.
I seem to have used up
all my good ideas.
What would Becky really like?

Wait a minute, Dad.
Look at my list.
What did you say first?

I said a tadpole,
then an elephant,
then an alligator.

A tadpole,
an elephant,
an alligator.
t – e – a .

Tea?
Yes, give her lots of tea.
I'll have it delivered
in a big truck.
Her mom will be pleased.

No Dad, it's Becky's birthday,
not her mom's birthday.
Can't you guess yet?
What else did you say?

Then I said a swan,
then an eel,
then a Tyrannosaurus Rex.

A swan,
an eel,
a Tyrannosaurus.
Have you got it now?
s − e − t .

Set?
A set of what?
A set of bagpipes?
Her mom will *not* be pleased.

It's tea set, Dad.
Together it spells tea set.
She would really like that.
Dad, you are not always silly.
Sometimes you are quite clever.

Thank you.
Any time you need help
with birthday presents,
just ask me.